Myth Quest
Jambavan

THE IMMORTAL BEAR

retold by Anu Kumar

illustrations by Maya Magical Studios

First published in 2011 by Hachette India
An Hachette UK company

www.hachetteindia.com

SRD

ISBN: 978-93-5009-286-6

Hachette India
612/614 (6th Floor), Time Tower
MG Road, Sector 28, Gurgaon 122001, India

Typeset in Adobe Garamond Pro 13/16 by
Eleven Arts, New Delhi

Printed and bound in India by
Manipal Technologies Limited, Manipal

Welcome to the world of MythQuest...

Discover the fables and legends about the origin, history, deities, ancestors and heroes of India.

While the term 'myth' in common conversation means a false story, in the world of religion, folklore and magic, myths are considered 'true'. They tell stories of the creation of the universe, the eternal battle between good and evil, and the history of humankind itself.

The main characters in our myths are bigger and better than any modern superheroes. They are birds and beasts, gods and demons, kings and queens, generals and warriors, sages and gurus, each with extraordinary powers that changed the course of history and the fate of the human race.

The people to whom a myth belongs consider it a true account of their past millions of years ago. Even today, they continue to worship the gods and goddesses, follow the rituals and read the texts that developed from these myths.

Hachette's MythQuest series brings to you fascinating stories from the vast treasures of ancient mythology. Read them all—and become a MythMaster!

Mythological characters and events have been described in different ways in different versions of ancient texts. We have chosen the most interesting and key stories to build a comprehensive account for the young reader.

This book is about . . .

. . . Jambavan, the great half-man and half-bear, who was the son of Brahma, the Creator of the Universe. Also known as Jambavantha or Jamvanta, this immortal bear is believed to have been born even before the universe was created.

A great devotee of Vishnu, the Preserver of the Universe, Jambavan came down to earth in order to help him fight against evil.

Jambavan appeared during the Ramayana to help Vishnu in his Rama avatar to confront and battle the wicked Ravana, king of the rakshasas. *He was also present when Vishnu took on his Vamana avatar, as well as when he was incarnated as Krishna as narrated in the Mahabharata.*

Said to be endowed with the strength of ten million lions and the wisdom and foresight of the gods themselves, Jambavan was a brilliant leader, an able strategist and a formidable opponent.

Here is Jambavan's story, jam-packed with action and adventure . . .

CHAPTER ONE

THE BIRTH OF JAMBAVAN

It was a time long ago, so far back, that one cannot even imagine it. It was a time before the world as we know it and any of the lands in it existed. The Great Flood had been released by the gods to destroy all the evil on earth and Vishnu had taken on his *matsya* or fish avatar to protect Manu—the only man who survived the flood and became the father of all humankind—and to ensure the continuance of the birds, beasts and plants.

It was just after the flood, while the waters were receding, that Brahma saw a beautiful lotus right in the middle of the waters. But, before he could do anything about it, Madhu and Kaithaba, two very powerful *asuras* arrived on the scene. They had been created from the ear wax of Lord Vishnu while he was in deep sleep. The mighty duo had grown so arrogant that they even challenged Brahma, the Creator of the Universe, to a fight and were intent on killing him.

Seeing them make threatening gestures, Brahma began to feel a little nervous. A drop of sweat rolled down his forehead and trickled down his body. Jambavan was created from this droplet of sweat. He emerged fully formed and floating on the waters that covered the earth.

There is another story describing the birth of Jambavan. Ravana, the wicked *rakshasa*, had been

plaguing the gods and they came to Vishnu and begged him for help. Lord Vishnu promised to bring an end to Ravana's tyranny by taking on a human form—that of Rama, Prince of Ayodhya, and defeating the ten-headed Lord of Lanka in battle.

Lord Brahma knew that Vishnu would require assistance in vanquishing Ravana as he was very powerful and so he decided to create the *vanara sena*, or the army of monkeys. Concentrating deeply, Brahma was about to create the first monkey when he suddenly yawned. And out of this yawn leaped out Jambavan, the great bear.

Thus Jambavan was born of the gods themselves and blessed with great strength and wisdom. He was one of the *chiranjeevis*, or immortal beings, who would live till the end of the world itself. Right from the time he was born, Jambavan started praying to Lord Vishnu, the Preserver of the Universe, and became a great worshipper of the god.

CHAPTER TWO

A TALE OF DEEP DEVOTION

A faithful devotee of Vishnu, Jambavan followed him in his journey across Heaven and earth through the different *yugas*, or ages in the history of the universe. Jambavan appeared on earth as Vishnu took on each of his ten avatars to rid the world of evil forces.

Jambavan was big and powerful, and stories of his strength abounded. Once when Vishnu appeared in his Vamana avatar, Jambavan performed such a marvellous feat that he amazed gods and humans alike.

The *asura* king Bali had grown very strong and had succeeded in defeating even Indra, the Lord of Heaven. All the gods turned to Brahma who advised them to pray to Lord Vishnu. On seeing their plight, he agreed to help them by taking on the Vamana avatar to punish the proud *asura* king.

Now Bali was holding a great sacrifice and, to mark the occasion, he was giving away gifts to all the holy men in the land. Vishnu knew that Bali was renowned for his generosity and he would never refuse anyone a gift.

Well disguised as a dwarf, Vamana made his way to Bali's palace and stood in line with the other sages. Bali looked at him kindly and said, 'Tell me your heart's desire, O Vamana, and I will give it to you.'

'All I want is three paces of land,' said Vamana meekly. All those present at the gathering suppressed their smiles and tried to persuade the diminutive man to ask for something else, but Vamana remained adamant. When Bali finally agreed, Vamana stepped forward and started growing right before his eyes.

He grew taller and taller, overshooting the biggest trees and the highest mountains. His legs thickened until they became like massive pillars that reached all the way into the clouds. Vamana had attained such massive proportions that his head was among the planets, and the stars. Earth looked like a tiny splotch of colour from such a height. He then lifted his gigantic feet and crossed earth and Heaven in two easy strides. Bali stood there, watching awestruck, and then offered his own head as Vamana had run out of land to cover with his third step. Thus Vamana placed his feet on Bali's head and pushed him down, down, down, right to the underworld.

All this while, Jambavan had been watching from a distance. He saw Vishnu's transformation from the tiny dwarf to the majestic Vamana who regained the worlds from the clutches of the *asura* king. This only reinforced his unending faith and devotion.

Overwhelmed by his Lord's divine countenance, he wished to offer obeisance to him. So Jambavan folded his hands and began his *pradakshina*—circumambulation as a form of worship—around Vamana. As he started circling Vamana, Jambavan himself began to grow taller and taller. In a few steps the great bear king completed three circles around Vamana and displayed his own strength and divinity to all.

CHAPTER THREE

THE SEARCH FOR SITA

Jambavan was one of the trusted advisers of the *vanara* prince, Sugriva, who had been exiled from his home at Kishkindha by his elder brother Vali, the king of the *vanaras*. Driven away from his home due to a misunderstanding, Sugriva now lived in the Rishyamukha Parvat with his followers.

It was here that he met Jambavan and they soon became fast friends. Sugriva trusted and admired this great king of bears. Jambavan had promised to help Sugriva defeat his brother Vali and return to Kishkindha as king. This further strengthened their bond.

One day, as the two of them sat together, Jambavan turned to Sugriva and said, 'Prince Rama can help you regain your kingdom and defeat your brother. You must strike a deal with him. Help him find his wife, Sita, who has been abducted by Ravana, the evil King of Lanka. In return, the prince will kill Vali and help you return to your home as king of the *vanaras*.'

Sugriva followed Jambavan's advice and approached Rama with his plan. The prince fulfilled his part of the deal and killed Vali in combat. Now, it was Sugriva's turn to make good his promise.

He requested his trusted friend Jambavan to call upon the bears as this was a difficult task for the *vanaras* alone. He also begged him to join the combined army as a general.

Jambavan was a great leader with a lot of power in the animal kingdom. He stood before the gathered troops of brave and strong bears and said, 'I call upon all the bears under my rule to join the search for Sita. We must give all we can to this mission as the great prince Rama needs our help to find his wife and defeat the wicked Ravana who has kidnapped her. I ask for volunteers to come forward and help me.'

Every bear in the kingdom bore great loyalty towards their king, and without hesitating for a minute, every single one of them stepped forward.

Jambavan smiled but cautioned them gently. 'I must warn you that this quest will lead to a bloody battle,' he said grimly. 'I cannot guarantee that all of you will come back unharmed or even alive.'

'We are ready,' chorused the bears, undeterred by Jambavan's grave words. Quickly, they trooped into files and followed their leader to Kishkindha to meet the *vanaras*. There they assembled as one, and thus merged, their forces were now twice as strong.

Sugriva stood up and addressed the gathered forces. 'I have given my word to Rama that we will get news of Sita no matter where she is. You must not come back without the information. I would rather see you dead than return empty-handed,' concluded Sugriva, and every member of the army knew that he meant every word he said.

The bears and the *vanaras* set off under the leadership of Jambavan and Hanuman, a senior and powerful *vanara* general. They scoured the land for every sign of Sita. They tried to follow the trail of jewels she had left behind while she was being carried away forcibly by Ravana. They also pondered over Jatayu's last words as the great king of birds had died after fighting bravely on Sita's behalf. But they couldn't find any clues that led to Sita's whereabouts.

The army left no corner of the land unsearched. But there was no sign of Sita or any other information that would lead them in the right direction. She seemed to have vanished into thin air! The bears and *vanaras* slowly grew more and more despondent.

At last they reached what seemed like the end of the world to them. The land jutted out into a vast ocean that surrounded it on three sides. Heavy boulders, as tall as hills, looked down on the sandy beach that was entirely isolated. Apart from the *vanara* army, the place was deserted for *yojanas* on end.

However, unknown to them, they were being watched by the giant bird Sampati. This creature was Jatayu's brother and had once been a magnificent bird with an unmatched flight. However, his wings had

been burnt by the Sun's blaze when he had once flown too close to it, racing with his brother, and since then Sampati lived here alone. His home was atop a mountain with a commanding view of the earth and the seas.

The great bird saw the *vanara* army gather below him and he was at first pleased at the prospect of such easy prey for his dinner.

However, then he noticed how tired and sad the *vanaras* looked. Moved by their condition, he decided to help them. He went down and asked them what the matter was. Once he came to know about their quest, Sampati gave the monkeys and the bears some very important news.

Perched on his spot high up on the mountain, he had seen something that no one else had. 'I have seen it all with my own eyes,' said Sampati. 'I saw Ravana take the lovely Sita in his flying chariot. It was moving as fast as the wind and they flew right past here, crossed the ocean and entered Lanka.'

After they heard Sampati's story, Jambavan and Hanuman took Sampati aside and gently broke the news of his brother Jatayu's death to him.

Despite the sadness at having lost Jatayu, the general atmosphere was one of jubilation as the army had received their first real lead to Sita's whereabouts.

CHAPTER FOUR

JAMBAVAN ASKS A QUESTION

Armed with the first solid bit of information they had received since they had set out, the army now resumed their search with new energy. Following Sampati's directions, they realized that Sita was being held captive in the island kingdom of Lanka. They also realized that to reach Lanka they would have to cross the entire stretch of the ocean.

Reaching the end of the land, the army came to a halt. Their faces fell and their enthusiasm vanished as they could suddenly go no further. The surging ocean on all sides made even the strongest bear and the most agile *vanara* quail in fear and indecision. They began to chatter and flail their arms in confusion.

Only Jambavan in his infinite wisdom knew the solution to the problem at hand.

He looked at the shimmering expanse of water, and he knew that it would take someone of exceptional skill and agility to jump across the ocean and reach Lanka. He also knew that this was not a task for any old bear or *vanara*. Only an exceptional *vanara* with special powers could do this.

Having made up his mind, Jambavan stepped forward and spoke in a calming manner. As he addressed the gathering, the chatter quietened and everyone began to listen intently.

'My friends,' said Jambavan, 'this is but a minor hurdle and I know the way to overcome it.' He was immediately greeted by cheers.

Gesturing for silence, he continued, 'This is a task for you, *vanaras*, as you are known for your ability to leap across large distances. This quest needs a few volunteers who will be ready to leap across the ocean and make their way to Lanka. Even one determined volunteer will do.'

The initial excitement was replaced by an uncomfortable silence. All faces fell and even the largest monkey cowered in fear. No one came forward. The ocean had made everyone lose hope. It stretched across more than a thousand *yojanas* and most *vanaras* knew attempting

a vault across it was well nigh impossible. They did not have the confidence to make such a crossing. Apart from this, they also feared the might of Ravana.

The most capable and important *vanaras* such as Gaja, Gavaaksha, Gavaya, Sharabha, Gandhamaadana, Susheshna, Mainda and Dvivida began to boast of their abilities, but none of them agreed to go as far as Lanka.

'I can fly thirteen *yojanas* and that is about it,' said Gaja, to which Gavaaksha responded by saying, 'I can go over twenty-five *yojanas* and I think that is a lot for any *vanara*.' Sharabha, another senior monkey, stood up saying, 'For my part, I can go up to thirty-eight *yojanas* but not more,' to which someone else said, 'Fifty *yojanas* and that's it'. Gandhamaadana, the most magnificently dressed of all the *vanaras*, said he could span a maximum of sixty-three *yojanas*. Mainda said that he had once ventured to leap up to seventy-five *yojanas* and managed, but that was the extent of his ability. Dvivida, another important *vanara*, stood up to his full height and told the assembly rather proudly that he could go up to eighty-eight *yojanas* and not a step more. The last one to speak among them was the very senior and greatly respected *vanara*, Susheshna, who added to the discussion by saying, 'I promise to jump a hundred *yojanas* . . .'

And so it went on and it seemed like it would never stop. Prince Angad, the son of Vali and the future *vanara* king, began to despair. He thought that their quest was doomed as even the most capable and important monkey generals had all failed him. They boasted of their prowess, but none of them agreed to take the chance and jump across the ocean.

Jambavan also listened to the empty braggadocio with a heavy heart. He wondered sadly about the passing of his own strength and skill. He remembered his glorious youth when he had walked around Lord Vishnu in his mighty Vamana avatar.

Now, he stood before the army of the most powerful

vanaras in the world and not one of them could or would try to leap across the ocean.

Finally, the young Prince Angad stood up and spoke. He mocked the other senior *vanaras* and said, 'I can bound across this ocean, but whether I am capable of coming back or not, I am not sure. But at least I could try.'

There was silence after he spoke. No one dared speak up as Angad was heir to the throne. However, he was young and impulsive, and it was left to Jambavan to dissuade him as it was too dangerous a mission for such a young *vanara*—especially one who was slated to be the future king.

'Great Prince, you are the best among us and I know that you are capable of making the leap,' said Jambavan flattering the young prince as well as convincing him to change his mind. 'A thousand *yojanas* are nothing and I am sure you can go much farther. But I have promised your uncle Sugriva that I will protect you at whatever cost and thus I cannot let you take such a risk,' concluded Jambavan.

Despite the confident words, in his heart Jambavan was unsure of the young Angad's abilities. He was also deeply concerned about their mission, which seemed to be teetering on the brink of uncertainty without a volunteer to cross the great ocean.

CHAPTER FIVE

JAMBAVAN REVEALS A SECRET

Despite all of Jambavan's personal concerns, the immediate task at hand for him was to dissuade the young prince from any hasty actions as he had himself taken the responsibility for the safety of Angad.

'I am now very old and decrepit,' he said. 'At best, I am an advisor rather than a soldier, and I can only help with the wisdom of my long years of experience. But in my youth, my energy and powers had impressed all.

Indeed, I was unsurpassed in my strength.' He paused with a faraway expression on his face.

'Now, at my advanced age, it is not possible for me to leap across an ocean and face a strong enemy on my own. And that is why I asked for a volunteer. However, it cannot be you as you are the future king and have responsibilities to fulfil.'

Disheartened by Jambavan's words, Angad said that then the *vanaras* had no choice but to kill themselves in shame. He reminded them of Sugriva's words and said, 'I do not think returning to Kishkindha will be any easier than trying to cross this ocean as we will all have to face the brunt of Sugriva's wrath.'

Suddenly, Jambavan spotted a lone *vanara* sitting on a rock and immediately his frown vanished and he smiled slightly.

'All is not lost,' he said to the gathering. 'I think I know what needs to be done. Just give me some time and I will return with good news.' With this Jambavan hurried away purposefully.

Now Jambavan knew something that no one else did—and this secret was going to be the key to the victory they hoped for.

He knew the truth about Hanuman.

While he was a senior leader in the army, that was merely a small part of Hanuman's other powers. And now when Jambavan spotted him sitting by himself on a boulder, he decided it was time for a revelation.

Jambavan was the only person who knew about Hanuman's limitless powers. In the midst of all the confusion, it had slipped his mind that Hanuman was no less than a god in the powers that he wielded and was the most valuable asset in the combined army of monkeys and bears.

It had come to him in a flash that the only *vanara* capable of crossing the ocean was Hanuman, the greatest of them all. The only thing stopping him was his own memory. Or the lack of it.

A curse had made Hanuman forget about his past life and his powers. As Jambavan walked up to him, he decided that it was time for Hanuman to remember who he really was. It was time to change the course of Ravana's fate by introducing their greatest strength into the fray.

Hanuman was lost in thought when Jambavan walked up to him. The all-wise Jambavan realized his problem at once. He knew that this great monkey was in a dilemma over fulfilling his duty and coming to terms with his indecision over crossing the ocean.

He also knew that Hanuman had met Rama earlier in the forest and had become his devoted friend and follower. Rama had given him a ring for Sita and he was bound by duty

to go to Lanka and give it to her. So Hanuman had joined the *vanara* army in order to achieve this task.

However, once they had reached the shore, there had been no further progress because the other *vanaras* kept arguing and debating without actually agreeing to take on the challenge of crossing the ocean.

Hanuman k
vanaras were he
they were mortal
Ravana's strength as
unknown territory
Hanuman himself
afraid of Ravana or
other *rakshasa*, but nor
confident of crossing the
in a single leap. Like all the o
vanaras, he too had reservatio
However, he was bound by h
promise. He had to deliver Rama
ring to Sita, and he knew he would have to go whether he could cross the ocean in a single leap or not.

If another more capable *vanara* volunteered to do the deed, then Hanuman would accompany him and fulfill his personal duty. So he waited on the boulder, hoping that the indecision among the *vanaras* would somehow resolve itself.

Jambavan knew all of this and decided that it was time for Hanuman to understand his true potential. Standing in front of the monkey general he began to speak softly. The bear king recounted from memory, stories and deeds that no other living being remembered.

'The time has come for you to remember your st, Great Hanuman. It is time to be the hero you ere always meant to be. Forget all the confusion nd uncertainty that the others are going through. O Hanuman, you are no ordinary *vanara*. You are the son of Vayu, the all-powerful God of Wind, and Anjana, the *apsara*-turned-*vanara* princess. You are also known as Pavanputra—the son of the Wind God, and are blessed with his magical powers. Thus you have the speed of the wind and you can fly in the sky as high and for as long as Garuda—the mount of Vishnu—himself. You are supposed to be an incarnation of Lord Shiva, who lost a wager to Vishnu and thus was born as a monkey to serve Rama.'

Jambavan's words shocked Hanuman into silence. He listened with rapt attention as the old bear continued with his tale:

'You are so powerful, O Divine Monkey, that you had once leapt towards the Sun, thinking it was a ripe mango. The gods were apprehensive and Indra, the Lord of Heaven, alarmed at your antics, had struck you with a thunderbolt. Although you fell and broke your jaw, you also managed to impress Indra with your show of daring and strength. The mighty thunderbolt that smote strong enemies had merely grazed you. Your father Vayu saw you injured and he blew up a furious gale, threatening to destroy all in his anger. The other gods tried to pacify, him and finally

Brahma stepped in to take control and appease the Wind God by granting you a boon.' Jambavan stopped to catch his breath.

'Don't you see?' he continued excitedly. 'Your power is limitless. For Lord Brahma's boon made you completely immune to any kind of missile or weapon. Lord Indra also granted you a boon whereby you could choose the time of your death and therefore are immortal if you so desire. These two boons have made you completely indestructible,' concluded Jambavan with a grand flourish.

Then the wise bear returned to the situation at hand. He pointed to himself saying, 'I am too old and my strength is not what it used to be. Even though I am still far stronger than many who are gathered here today, it is you who are the chosen one. Your might and divine gifts have made you the most powerful and agile among all of us and it is you who must make this leap across the ocean.'

Jambavan's words brought about a transformation in the otherwise quiet and withdrawn *vanara*. Armed with a new confidence, he immediately volunteered to make the jump across the great ocean to Lanka.

CHAPTER SIX

THE BATTLE BEGINS

Finally, through his infinite wisdom, Jambavan managed to end the confusion in the *vanara* army and save the mission to find Sita. His words had spurred Hanuman into action and he now grew to gigantic proportions right before the eyes of all who were assembled. Then, in one huge leap he flew off towards Lanka.

Once there, he found Sita in the Ashok Vatika, a garden in Ravana's kingdom, and gave her Rama's ring and she gave him a necklace for her lord. However, she refused to leave with Hanuman, because she felt that the only honourable way would be for her husband to fight Ravana and win her back.

While he was talking to Sita, Hanuman was suddenly discovered and captured by Ravana's men. The *rakshasa* king then ordered his deputies to set Hanuman's tail on fire. However, the great monkey with his superhuman powers was not an easy one to keep imprisoned and he escaped and flew all across Lanka, wreaking great havoc with his blazing tail.

Finally, leaving a trail of destruction in his wake,

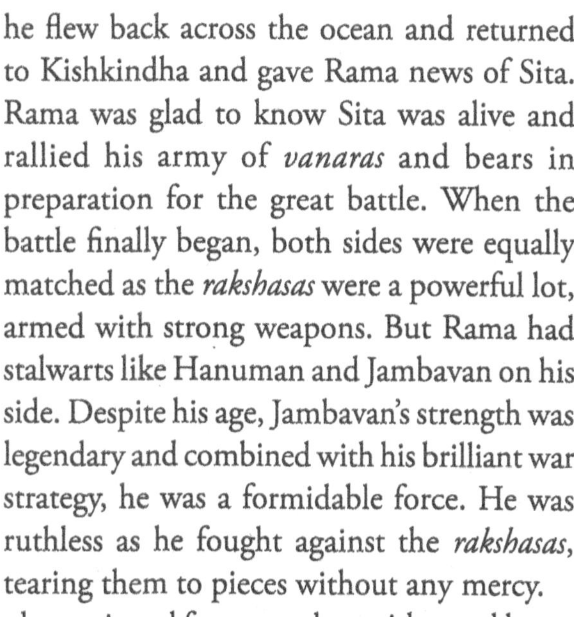

he flew back across the ocean and returned to Kishkindha and gave Rama news of Sita. Rama was glad to know Sita was alive and rallied his army of *vanaras* and bears in preparation for the great battle. When the battle finally began, both sides were equally matched as the *rakshasas* were a powerful lot, armed with strong weapons. But Rama had stalwarts like Hanuman and Jambavan on his side. Despite his age, Jambavan's strength was legendary and combined with his brilliant war strategy, he was a formidable force. He was ruthless as he fought against the *rakshasas*, tearing them to pieces without any mercy.

The battle continued for many days with equal losses on both sides. During the peak of the battle, Jambavan came face to face with Ravana himself. He moved with a speed and fought with a ferocity that was unbelievable for his age. He lashed out with his bare hands and gave Ravana such mighty blows that the king reeled backwards. Finally, Jambavan kicked Ravana on his chest with his powerful legs, rendering him unconscious.

Ravana fell back against his chariot and his charioteer raced back to the palace with him before he could come to further harm and lose the war. This temporary victory gave Rama's army an upper hand—at least for a while.

CHAPTER SEVEN

JAMBAVAN SAVES THE DAY

The battle with Ravana's army was long-drawn and fortunes swung from one side to the other on a daily basis. One day, Ravana sent his most formidable warrior into battle. This was his son, Meghnad. Armed with several boons from Lord Brahma, which included a quiver of neverending arrows, an invincible bow, the power of invisible flight and an indestructible flying chariot, Meghnad was one of the most powerful *rakshasas*.

Once Ravana had attacked Indra and was defeated and captured. Then, Meghnad had joined the battle and vanquished Indra himself with his great powers. As a result of this, he was also known as Indrajit—the one who has gained victory over Indra.

Kumbhakarna, Ravana's younger brother, had just died at the hands of Rama and so Indrajit comforted his distraught father by promising to wreak a terrible revenge and kill both Rama and Lakshmana.

Armed with several celestial weapons including the *nagapasha* or the serpent noose and the extremely powerful

Brahmastra—the deadliest weapon created by Brahma—which eventually failed him as it could only be used to uphold the cause of *dharma*—the rules that laid down what was right and what was wrong, Indrajit wreaked havoc among the *vanara* soldiers. He fought Jambavan in a strongly contested battle and finally defeated him as he could remain invisible while he fought, thereby gaining an upper hand. Indrajit also defeated Sugriva, Angad and the other chiefs in the same manner. He also engaged in furious combat with Lakshmana and, finally, knocked him unconscious with a powerful arrow.

As dusk approached, Rama grew worried because he had had no news of Lakshmana. He sent Vibhishana—Ravana's youngest brother who had come over to their side—and Hanuman to inspect the battlefield. They searched all over and came across thousands of slain and wounded *vanaras* till they finally chanced upon Lakshmana. His breath was very faint and he looked close to death.

A little further on, Vibhishana came across another figure lying on the ground. It was Jambavan, the king of bears, who had been felled in the battle with Indrajit. Leaning close, Vibhishana asked if he was alive, for he feared the worst. Recognizing Vibhishana's voice, Jambavan mustered all his strength to ask a question. 'Is Hanuman still alive?' he whispered.

A relieved but surprised Vibhishana responded, 'O Great Bear, how come you do not ask about our great leaders Rama or Lakshmana, but enquire about Hanuman first?'

Jambavan took in big gulps of air as he was quite weak. His massive chest heaved with the effort it took to speak. 'This is because I know that the divine Rama will be safe,' he whispered. 'But without Hanuman and his great powers, we are truly lost.'

Hanuman, who had also arrived on the scene, was delighted when he saw that Jambavan was alive. He bowed low in respect and touched the great bear's feet. Jambavan too rejoiced when he saw Hanuman was indeed safe despite Indrajit's onslaught. He gritted his teeth, for his wounds were quite severe, and proceeded to give Hanuman some very important instructions:

'Once again, Hanuman, it is only you who can save all of us, including Lakshmana, whose life is fast ebbing. You have to fly over the sea again and make your way to the Dronagiri Parvat in the high Himalayas and return with the life-giving herb called *sanjeevani booti*.'

The all-wise Jambavan explained that this rare herb, which only grew on those mountains, had special powers. Apart from the gods, he was one of the few who knew about the existence of the *sanjeevani* herb and the fact that it could restore to life all those who had been injured and were close to death.

Hanuman immediately raced across the sky till he reached Dronagiri Parvat. However, once he was there, he found he could not identify the correct herb despite Jambavan's accurate description. He also knew that he was running out of time, so he lifted up the entire mountain in one hand and returned with it to Lanka!

When Hanuman reached Lanka, he was welcomed by the surviving *vanaras*. Jambavan immediately identified the correct herb and its leaves were made into a special potion. While some of the *vanaras* were healed by the fragrance of the herb itself, others who were more seriously injured, like Lakshmana, were revived instantly after imbibing the potion. Jambavan himself was restored to his normal strength by the magical potion.

The bitter and heavily contested war finally came to an end, with heavy losses on both sides. However, Rama emerged victorious and Ravana met a bitter end. Jambavan's able leadership had guided Rama's army, and his astute wisdom and helped save the day on more than one occasion, finally helping Rama win the war.

This is not where Jambavan's story ends, though. He also appeared on earth along with Vishnu in his later avatars. Notably among them was his presence in Dwarka during the time of the Mahabharata when Vishnu came to earth in his eighth avatar—Krishna.

CHAPTER EIGHT

JAMBAVAN AND KRISHNA

The immortal bear always assisted Vishnu in whatever way possible in his fight against evil. Thus when Vishnu came to earth as Krishna, Jambavan was also incarnated as the king of bears whose home was in the forest near Dwarka. However, this time Jambavan was unaware of Krishna's true identity.

Krishna had made Dwarka his home and established his own kingdom there with his Yadava subjects from Mathura. Although Krishna was greatly loved and respected by most of his people, there were also those who resented his popularity. Some also blamed Krishna

for their banishment from Mathura by King Jarasandha. He was the uncle of Kamsa, the tyrant of Mathura, who had been killed by Krishna. Ever since that incident, Jarasandha had become a sworn enemy of the Yadavas.

Among the Yadavas opposed to Krishna was Satrajit, who was head of an important clan. Satrajit's daughter, Satyabhama, had, however, given her heart to Krishna ever since she had seen him defeat Kamsa—his evil uncle and ruler of the Vrishni kingdom with its capital at Mathura—in a wrestling match. But she did not dare mention it to her father as Satrajit was jealous of the loyalty and devotion that Krishna commanded from the Yadavas, and hated him.

Satrajit was a powerful prince

who lived in a palatial house in Dwarka. He was doted on by his kinsmen, and served by a retinue of followers. He also owned the precious Syamantakmani, a gem gifted to him by the the Sun God, Surya. It was believed that there was a sacred cave dedicated to the Sun God, located deep in the forest. Satrajit had once performed a long penance there and as a result of his devotion, the Sun God had presented him with the Syamantakmani.

The gem was housed in a temple dedicated to Surya and was zealously guarded at all hours. It was said Satrajit himself slept on the temple steps every night to stave off the possibility of the gem being stolen.

Unaware of his daughter's feelings for Krishna, Satrajit dreamt of cementing his position among the Yadavas by arranging a marriage between his daughter and Satyaki, the son of another powerful Yadava chieftain.

However, Satyabhama had other plans. She kidnapped Satyaki and spirited him away to a secret hiding place where she told him of her father's intentions and her own reasons for capturing him. She needed Satyaki's help in winning Krishna's hand—and she also knew a very important secret.

Earlier that very night, the Syamantakmani had been stolen. Satyabhama knew that her father would immediately suspect Krishna. And she had to help Krishna absolve himself of the crime.

Satrajit treasured the gem beyond all else and believed that it was the source of his power, fortune and greatness. When he realised that the gem was lost, Satrajit was distraught. His distress deepened when he found out that his daughter Satyabhama and Satyaki were also missing. He thought that they had eloped and, in his rage, he blamed Krishna for all the misfortunes that had befallen him all of a sudden. He even complained to the Yadava king, Ugrasena, saying that Krishna was jealous of him and desired his humiliation and had, therefore, stolen the gem and incited his daughter to run away.

When Krishna heard this, he immediately left Dwarka in search of the gem. Meanwhile, Satyabhama managed to convince Satyaki to help her, and together with her cat Uri, they rode into the forest in search of the gem.

Now this was the same forest that Jambavan lived in and ruled over and he did not take kindly to intruders. All the bears in his jungle were his guards and they dealt with all trespassers in a strict manner.

Satyabhama was very observant and had seen her father's brother Prasenjit ride off into the forest on the night of the theft. Her father came here every few days to pray to the Sun God and it was most unlike him to send someone on his behalf. When the gem's disappearance came to light, her worst fears were confirmed.

Satyabhama and Satyaki had not gone very far when, much to their horror, they discovered Prasenjit lying dead by the path. What caught their attention was a piece of golden string that dangled limply by his side and Satyabhama immediately recognized it as the string that had carried the Syamantakmani.

Whoever had killed Prasenjit had also stolen the Syamantakmani.

The two had barely gone any further when they were attacked by a sloth of bears. While Satyaki was taken forcibly away by the bears, Satyabhama ran for her dear life, but the thick bramble-ridden forests proved too much for her. She knew she was in the land of the bears, and that Jambavan did not like strangers. In her fear, she lost her balance and rolled down a rocky hillside. Bruised and battered, she lay in a gully at the very bottom of the hill.

Satyabhama would have surely died had it not been for the presence of her faithful cat Uri who had also accompanied her on this perilous journey into the forest.

There was another person on the trail of the Syamantakmani. It was none other than Lord Krishna, who had entered this dangerous forest in order to find the sacred jewel and find the real culprit.

Krishna had followed the same path and seen Prasenjit's body, the gold chain bereft of the jewel that was hanging by his side and the footsteps of the mountain lion that led away from it. While he was following this second pair of footprints, Krishna heard the loud meowing of a cat and he took a short detour off the main path to investigate.

Making his way through the thick brambles, he stumbled on to a strange scene. There was a cat trying to escape the attack of a snake. Krishna immediately smote the snake down and the cat scampered over to Krishna's side. This cat was no other than Uri. Rubbing her head against Krishna's leg in gratitude, she began to tug at the prince's clothes. Puzzled by her behaviour, Krishna finally realized that she was pulling him in a particular direction. He followed her till he reached the mouth of a ravine. Looking down, he could just about discern the shape of a woman. She was lying at the very bottom of the hill and was seriously injured as she lay completely motionless.

Krishna quickly climbed down and picked up the half-conscious form and carried her up the rocky precipice. Once on top, he looked at her closely and realized that it was none other than Satyabhama.

Gradually, she regained consciousness and recounted her story to him. Krishna then tended to her wounds and helped her up on her feet.

Realizing that they had a very important mission at hand, Krishna, Satyabhama and Uri made their way back to the trail. Despite her injuries, Satyabhama refused to turn back or abandon the search as she was determined to help her beloved Krishna clear his name.

CHAPTER NINE

INSIDE JAMBAVAN'S CAVE

After rescuing Satyabhama, Krishna continued with her on the search for the precious Syamantakmani. He returned to the point in the trail where he had seen Prasenjit's dead body. Right next to the dead man were traces of fur and teeth marks of a mountain lion, along with the empty gold chain that used to carry the gem.

He started following the trail, and soon after, he came across another carcass. A mountain lion lay dead and leading away from the body was a set of footprints which distinctly resembled those of a bear.

Krishna followed the footprints and reached a huge cave. He had heard rumours about the great bear king who lived in this jungle and guessed that this was Jambavan's lair and right outside it Krishna saw the bear king's son playing with the famous Syamantakmani.

Krishna realized that it was Jambavan who had killed the lion and taken the gem from him. He sounded his

conch shell, challenging Jambavan to a fight and entered the cave. Right in front of Krishna stood the biggest and fiercest looking bear he had ever seen. And he knew at once that it was the great bear king himself.

The all-knowing Jambavan knew that Krishna and Satyabhama had been in his forest for some time now and he knew that they were looking for the Syamantakmani. However, Jambavan had no intention of returning the beautiful jewel that he had gifted to his son as a plaything.

The two formidable opponents clashed in fearsome combat which lasted for twenty-eight days. They fought with weapons, rocks and even uprooted trees. Although Jambavan possessed superhuman strength, he was no match for Krishna.

At the end of the twenty-eight days, Jambavan finally realized that Krishna was no ordinary prince but a divine incarnation of Vishnu. A great devotee of the Lord, Jambavan was ashamed at having entered into combat with him. He immediately stopped fighting and accepted his defeat.

To make amends, he offered his daughter Jambavati's hand in marriage to Krishna and gave him the Syamantakmani as well. Despite battling with his beloved god, Jambavan indirectly resolved a great mystery, helped clear Krishna's name and brought the conflict with Satrajit to a peaceful end.

MythNotes

Jambavan still has a select group of dedicated devotees. These are the Madigas, a tribe in the state of Andhra Pradesh, who are traditional leather workers. However, in traditional societies, the Madigas were discriminated against due to their connection with leather which was considered unclean. The Madigas have always considered Jambavan to be their first ancestor and supreme god. The story of Jambavan as told in the Jambu Purana is narrated by this tribe through a dance form called the Yakshagana. This musical dance-drama highlights the importance of this tribe by tracing their roots to Jambavan, and elevates them from their downtrodden position in society.

Jambavan is believed to have emerged before the earth and the Heavens by the Madigas. They also believe that he was the originator of the heavenly trio of Brahma, Vishnu and Shiva and thus the foremost among the heavenly beings. It is believed that he created the other gods and celestial beings through the goddess Shakti and populated Heaven.

Jambhavan's dwelling place is identified as modern-day Jamvanta, a small town in Ratlam district in the state of Madhya Pradesh. Excavations have revealed traces of very ancient dwelling sites here.